A LEEG
OF HIS OWN

Failure to Lunch

NOX PRESS
books for that extra kick to give you more power
www.NoxPress.com

A LEEG OF HIS OWN

Failure to Lunch

Elise Leonard

NOX PRESS

books for that extra kick to give you more power

www.NoxPress.com

Leonard, Elise
A Leeg of His Own (a series) / Failure to Lunch
ISBN: 978-1-935366-10-2

First Nox Press printing: March 2009
Second Nox Press printing: September 2010

NOX PRESS

books for that extra kick to give you more power

This dedication is *long* overdue.

I am dedicating this book to my family.
My wonderful husband, John,
and my two amazing sons, Michael and John.

Without you, John, Nox Press would not exist.
It was with your encouragement and assistance that I had
the nerve to start this publishing house.
I want to thank you for your unquestioned support.
You are a *truly* good man,
and I am lucky that you love me as you do.

My sons also deserve my deep-felt thanks.
Michael and John, you have sacrificed a ***lot***
so I could start Nox Press.
I am blessed to have two sons who are selfless and giving
enough to tell me to start a business that will help people
enjoy reading and find literacy,
even when you ***knew*** that it would mean that you could
not have the "things" that your friends had
or go to the colleges of your choice.
You have sacrificed much so we could help others enjoy
the written word and have a better life through literacy.
You make me very, *very* proud!
And I am even *more* proud of the men you have become.

Special thanks to Daniel Shippey, the photographer who
took the cover picture for this book.
You are an amazing, talented photographer, Daniel.
Your work is fantastic!

~Elise

CHAPTER 1

"Why should we care?" Tyrone asked Ms. Gold.

"Why shouldn't you?" Ms. Gold asked back.

"Because the dude lived in the 1800s!" Tyrone argued.

We waited for Ms. Gold's response.

She looked around the room and sighed deeply.

"Look, guys, I think you'll be surprised," she said.

I didn't know about that.

It took a *lot* to surprise us.

"Just do it," she urged. "Choose a favorite. Then we'll talk. Okay?"

She made bug eyes at Tyrone.

If she could get Tyrone to do it? Then she'd pretty much have it made.

Tyrone was the hardest sell in the class.

"We have six computers," Ms Gold said. "So get in groups of five."

I raised my hand.

"Andrew?" Ms. Gold asked. "You have a question?"

"Yeah. You just want us to get online and get a quote?"

"Yes," she said. "Then jot it down."

"That's it?" Tyrone asked.

Ms. Gold tried not to smile.

She failed.

"Yes, Tyrone. That's it."

"One quote?" he asked.

"One quote," she repeated.

Tyrone rolled his eyes.

"You *know* this is going to turn into something more. Right?" Tyrone muttered to himself.

That made *me* smile.

"She never just gives us something like this, and then… that's all," Tyrone kept muttering.

He did that a lot.

Muttered to himself.

Being so close? I could always hear him. But no one else could.

I sat down at a computer.

"It starts out like this. And then *bang*! We're talking about reports. And papers. And projects," he kept muttering.

I pulled up a page of quotes.

It seemed Henry David Thoreau had a *lot* of quotes.

"Ah, Tyrone?" I said.

He turned his face my way.

"I've got some quotes here," I said.

Tyrone sat down next to me.

"*Dang*!" he yelled. "We've got to read 164 of 'em?!"

That made me laugh.

"She only wants one quote, Tyrone. Just read a few, pick one, and be done with it," I said.

"Good," he said. "'Cause there was no *way* I was reading 164 of 'em."

Tyrone moved his chair closer to the computer.

But he kept muttering to himself as he did it.

"What did the guy do? Stand around all day? Saying stuff? And make other people write it down?!"

Tyrone was funny.

Even when he wasn't trying to be.

"Oh this is nice," Katie said. She was at the next computer.

"Which one?" Sharon asked.

"*Be true to your work, your word, and your friend*," Katie answered.

"That *is* nice," Sharon said.

Tyrone got annoyed. "Would you two be quiet?! I'm trying to *read* here!"

"Don't hurt yourself," Bianca said with a giggle.

Tyrone waved her off.

Two minutes later, Tyrone whooped.

"I've got mine," he said.

He wrote it down and slid his chair back to his desk.

"Okay," he told Ms. Gold. "I'm ready to talk."

Ms. Gold smiled widely. "Okay, Tyrone. Just wait a few minutes. I'd like everyone to have a quote."

Tyrone nodded.

He folded his paper up into a little square.

"Mine's good," he said loudly.

Ms. Gold nodded. "So you found something you can relate to?"

Tyrone nodded. "Sure did."

"Even though the guy lived in the 1800s?" she asked.

"After I read some of his stuff, he wasn't so bad," Tyrone confessed.

"For a dude from the 1800s," Ms. Gold added.

Tyrone nodded. "He was probably ahead of his time."

Ms. Gold smiled.

Four minutes later, everyone had a quote.

The quiet girl in the back read hers first.

"*All good things are wild, and free*," she said softly.

"And why do you like that quote?" Ms. Gold asked her.

She shrugged. "I like animals. They're good. Better than people."

"Okay," Ms. Gold said. "Anyone else?"

Another girl raised her hand.

Ms. Gold nodded at her. "Go ahead, Tiffany."

Tiffany spoke loudly. "*Go confidently in the direction of your dreams. Live the life you've imagined.*"

"And why did you pick that quote?" Ms. Gold asked.

"Because I'm going to go on American Idol. And I'm going to win it!"

Wow. Talk about going confidently!

"Okay, then," Ms. Gold said with a wide smile.

"Good luck with that."

Tiffany giggled piercingly.

If she sang anything like she giggled? Let's just say she was going to have a hard time on Idol.

"I guess Tiffany would hate my quote," Carlo said.

"And which quote did you choose?" Ms. Gold asked.

"*Rather than love, than money, than fame, give me truth*."

"Excellent," Ms. Gold said.

"I want to be a judge," Carlo explained.

Ms. Gold nodded. "Very good. Anyone else want to share?" she asked.

There were lots of hands raised. But Ms. Gold was probably curious.

"What about you, Tyrone?" she asked.

He unfolded his paper square.

It took, like, five minutes.

When he was done, he looked around to make sure everyone was listening.

He cleared his throat.

He thumped his chest with his fist.

He coughed a few times.

"Tyrone?" Ms. Gold said.

"Yeah?" Tyrone asked.

"Can you tell us some time in *this* century?" she asked.

He nodded seriously.

Then he looked around again.

He wanted everyone's attention.

"*It is never too late to give up your prejudices*," he read clearly.

Ms. Gold nodded. "Good one."

"They had prejudice back then?" Tyrone asked.

Ms. Gold answered simply. "Sadly, there has always been prejudice, Tyrone. There are many different *types* of prejudice. Unfortunately, there's still prejudice today, too."

Tyrone nodded. "I hear you, Ms. Gold. I hear you."

James raised his hand. "I like my quote."

"Which did you choose?" Ms. Gold asked him.

"*Any fool can make a rule, and any fool will mind it*," he said with a chuckle.

"That's true," Tyrone laughed.

We went around the room and just about everyone said their quote.

It was weird, but just about everyone picked something different.

I hadn't expected that.

"What was your quote, Andrew?" Ms. Gold asked me.

I read my quote. "*The man who goes alone can start today. But he who travels with another must wait till that other is ready*."

"What's that mean?" Rachel Morgan asked aloud.

Ms. Gold looked at me to explain.

"I think it means that if you're going to do something? You should probably do it alone. Because if you depend on others? You're going to have to wait for them."

I looked at Ms. Gold.

"Very well said," she said with a smile and a nod.

Little did I know just how true that saying was!

CHAPTER 2

The cafeteria was packed. And as noisy as always.

"Yeah. We had to do the same thing," Raul said.

"What was your favorite quote?" I asked him.

He leaned to his side and took a piece of paper from his back pocket.

He'd folded it up, too. Like Tyrone had done. Only Raul's was a triangle.

It looked like one of those paper footballs we used to make.

You know the ones.

The one's you flick with your finger? While the other person makes a little goal out of *his* hands?

You've got to flick it between the finger goalposts.

Raul read his quote. "*Success usually comes to those who are too busy to be looking for it.*"

"Boy. That Thoreau guy sure did say some stuff," I said as I took a bite of my English muffin pizza.

I opened my little box of chocolate milk and stuck in the straw.

Raul was busy lining up his Tater-Tots.

He had to count them.

I don't know why. It's just his thing.

He did that every time we had Tater-Tots.

"It's going to be a good day!" Raul said with joy.

"Got extra?" I asked.

If he got extra? It would be a good day.

If he got less than his average count? A bad day.

"Yup," he said happily. "One more than usual!"

I know it sounds stupid, but it was Raul's thing. And I was happy for him.

"That's great, Raul," I said honestly.

I looked around.

"Where's Snoop?" I asked as I finished off my English muffin pizza.

Raul shrugged. "I don't know."

"He's late," I noted.

"Yes," Raul agreed.

"That's not like Snoop," I added.

Raul shook his head. "No, it's not. Snoop's *never* late for lunch."

"It's his favorite class!" I said with a short laugh.

By the time I finished my chocolate milk and my peanut butter cookie? I *knew* something was wrong!

I ran over to my sister Abbie's table.

She sat with all the cool kids.

The jocks and stuff.

The popular table.

"Hey, Abbie," I said. "Have you seen Snoop?"

She looked up from her friends. "What?"

"Have you seen Snoop?" I repeated.

"Why would I?" she asked.

There were titters all around. Like she'd just said something *very* witty.

"I don't know," I said. "I just want to know if you've seen him."

Abbie went back to eating.

"Seen who?" Abbie asked.

"Stay with me, here," I told her. "Try to pay attention. Okay?!"

She sighed loudly and rolled her eyes.

"Just spit out what you want, Andy-boy," she said with impatience.

I hated when she called me Andy-boy.

It *really* annoyed me!

But there were more important things going on right now.

"Have you seen *Snoop*?!" I asked again.

She looked at me and smirked.

"Nope," she said. "It's not my day to watch him."

God, she was annoying.

I was about to tell her how annoying she was, but I had to find Snoop.

Which is a good thing for her!

(I would have eaten her alive!)

I ran over to the nerd table next.

That's where my other sister ate.

"Annie," I said.

She looked up from her math book.

Failure to Lunch

"Have you seen Snoop?" I asked.

"No, sorry. Is he lost?" she asked.

"He didn't show up for lunch," I said.

She laughed. "That's a first."

"I know," I told her. "That's why I'm worried."

She nodded.

"Where do you think he is?" she asked.

She was really smart, *most* of the time.

"If I knew that, I wouldn't be *asking* you!" I returned quickly.

She nodded again. "Right."

"Have you seen him at all today?" I asked her.

"I saw him in the hall. This morning," she said slowly.

She was thinking.

"I think it was before third period," she finished.

Hm. Okay.

So that meant he was here for first and second period.

"What does he have third period?" Annie asked me.

"Gym class," I said.

Annie smiled. "His second favorite class."

"Yeah," I agreed. "After lunch, that is."

Annie thought for a few seconds. "Do you think he made it to gym class?"

I shrugged. "Beats me."

"You'll have to ask around," Annie said.

I nodded. "Yeah. Okay, thanks."

I took off.

"Sorry I couldn't help you more," Annie called to my

back.

She was the good sister.

I had two. Annie and Abbie.

Annie was the sweet one.

Abbie was the evil one.

Oh yeah, and I was also their twin, in a way.

We're triplets.

Yeah. That's right.

There are three of us.

But as you can tell, only two of us are, well, human.

I went back to my table.

"Any news?" Raul asked.

He was popping his second to last Tater-Tot into his mouth.

"Not really," I said. "Annie thinks she saw him before third period."

"He's got gym then," Raul noted as he grabbed his last Tater-Tot.

"I know. We need to find someone in his gym class to see if he was there," I said.

Raul popped the last Tater-Tot in his mouth. "Know anyone?"

"Not really. You?" I asked Raul.

"No."

"Well it can't hurt to ask around," I said.

I turned to the table next to ours.

"Any of you guys have gym with Snoop?" I asked loudly.

Failure to Lunch

Lunchtime was always a bit loud. It was the only time we got to talk.

And boy could some of us talk!

Most of the people shook their heads and said no. But one girl gave us something to go on.

"I think he's in my friend Geetha's gym class," she said. "Let me go ask her."

"Mind of I come along?" I asked.

She shrugged. "No."

We walked to another table.

A table filled with girls.

They were all talking at the same time.

I wondered if any of them were listening. To anything!

The girl I was with just talked over the chatting group. "Geetha?"

A girl looked up. "Yes?"

"Is Snoop in your gym class?" I asked her.

"Yes," she said slowly.

She was eyeing me with distrust.

"Was he there today?" I asked her.

"Yes… and no," she said.

Yes and no? What the heck does *that* mean?!

"Well which was it?" I asked Geetha.

"It was both," she said.

"He was either *there* or he wasn't," I corrected loudly.

She shrugged off my comment.

Then she turned back toward her friends.

"Wait," I said quickly.

I tried to calm down.

I needed answers. I had to get her to explain what she was talking about.

Yelling at her wasn't going to get me anywhere.

I knew that.

So I took a deep breath and tapped her shoulder.

"Um, Geetha?" I said with a calm smile. "I don't get what you're trying to tell me."

She rolled her eyes and sighed.

Then she looked at her friends.

They rolled their eyes and smiled at Geetha. Supporting her through this tough time.

The time she had to speak to an idiot.

"*First* he was there," she said slowly. "And *then* he was gone."

CHAPTER 3

"Was he in class?" I asked Geetha.

"No," she said. "I saw him before class. By the water fountain."

"Which water fountain?" I asked.

"The one by the *gym*," she said with annoyance.

"So he was right there?" I asked.

"Yes."

"Right outside the gym?" I posed.

"Yes."

"Right before class?" I mentioned.

"That's right," she said as if I needed to be locked up at the crazy farm.

"But he didn't show up for class," I said.

She sighed heavily. "That's what I've been trying to *tell* you!"

"And you didn't think anything was *fishy*?" I asked.

She rolled her eyes again.

Her friends giggled.

"Guys are *always* doing stupid things," one of her friends piped in.

"Yeah," another added. "Guys are *not* logical!"

"Who can *tell* what they're trying to do?!" a third

supplied.

"They're all idiots," three of them chorused.

What was this? The local chapter of the Guy-Hating club?!

I wondered if my sister Abbie was a card-carrying member.

Who was I kidding?! She was probably their leader!

I tried to get out of there whole.

They were working themselves up. Getting all out of joint.

If I had to guess? I'd have to say this was all thanks to Billy Walsh.

Billy Walsh used to go out with one of Geetha's friends. Then he dumped her.

For some cheerleader girl.

Turns out the cheerleader girl didn't even *like* Billy Walsh.

She was just messing with him.

So then Billy Walsh tried to get back with Geetha's friend.

But she was too hurt by the whole thing.

Which I could understand.

But, hey. *I* wasn't Billy Walsh!

And I wasn't the one who hurt Geetha's friend.

And I didn't think it was right that all guys should suffer for one guy's stupidity.

But this table of girls hadn't gotten around to my way of thinking yet.

They were still pretty ticked off at guys, in general.

So I needed to escape quickly. Before they swarmed.

"Okay. Well, thanks for the info," I said with a smile.

They all stared at me. Fuming.

"If anyone sees Snoop, just give me a holler, okay?" I asked weakly.

I think my voice cracked a little.

I turned and ran away, headed back for the safety of my table with Raul.

I could hear laughter floating on the airwaves behind me.

Oh well. Better them laughing at me than killing me.

"So what did you find out?" Raul asked me as I stumbled back to the table.

I answered his question with a question.

"You know how you and I always wonder why girls don't really care for us too much?" I asked him.

He looked down at the table. "Yeah. What about it?"

"I think we should be grateful," I answered honestly.

I saw Raul's eyes dart over to my sister Annie's table.

Well, not really her *table*. Her. Annie.

"What makes you say that?" he asked me.

"I almost got attacked by a gang of angry girls," I explained. "For no good reason!"

"Well what did you do to them?" he asked me.

See? Guys could be logical.

Maybe not me *personally*. But *Raul* was logical.

"I didn't do anything to them," I complained. "I just

23

asked about Snoop."

"So what did you find out?" Raul asked.

"That Billy Walsh *really* hurt one of Geetha's friends."

"The one he dumped for that cheerleader?"

"Yeah," I answered.

"The cheerleader that didn't even *like* him?" Raul went on.

What was it with this school?! Were we all a bunch of gossiping hyenas?

Didn't we have better things to do with our time?

Well, maybe not.

There really wasn't that much for kids our age to do.

Particularly when we were in school.

But really?!

What *was* this? The set for Desperate Schoolgirls?

I wondered if every school was like this.

You know, filled with drama.

"Can we get back to the subject?" I asked Raul.

He looked confused.

"*Snoop*!" I bellowed.

"Oh. Yeah. What did you find out about him?" Raul asked.

He snuck one last peek at Annie, then gave me his full attention.

"He was at the water fountain before gym class," I started. "Then he didn't show up for class."

"So something must have happened while he was

getting a drink," Raul stated with certainly.

"Ya *think*?!" I shrieked.

"Yes," he said simply. "But what do *you* think happened?"

"If I *knew* that, I'd know where Snoop was," I hollered. "Wouldn't I?"

Raul wasn't sensing my frustration.

"I suppose," he said plainly.

The bell rang and it was time to move on to the second half of the day.

I threw out my paper plates and tiny milk carton. But throwing away my fears for what happened to Snoop wasn't as easy.

I don't think I heard a thing that was said for the rest of the day.

I hoped it wasn't important stuff. Because if it was? I didn't catch any of it.

But finally, the end of school came.

It certainly took its sweet time getting there!

I was off the bus, walking home, thinking about Snoop.

I wondered where he'd gone.

I wondered if he was okay.

I wondered if he were hurt.

Why else would he miss both gym class and lunch?

Maybe I should call my mom at the hospital to see if he'd been admitted.

She worked there. As a nurse.

I was deep in thought, when out of the blue, something hit me.

It scared the heck out of me.

I almost wet my pants.

I mean, there I was, walking home alone, deep in thought. Then, out of nowhere, something hits me.

I looked around.

Nothing.

Annie was at a math club meeting.

Abbie was at swim practice.

It was just me.

Alone.

With my thoughts.

And a…

I looked around.

A big hunk of grass was lying at my feet.

Now how did *that* happen?!

Hunks of grass don't just go flying through the air like that. Did they?

I looked around again.

Another hunk of grass was careening my way.

Dang! Look at that!

Hunks of grass *could* fly through the air.

This one hit me on the cheek.

I was spitting and sputtering, trying to get any flying dirt out of my mouth.

"Andrew!" I heard someone whisper.

I looked around.

Failure to Lunch

I saw nothing.

And nobody.

"Andrew!" someone whispered louder.

It sounded a little like Snoop. But I couldn't see him.

"Snoop?" I said aloud. "Is that you?"

"Who *else* would it be?!" Snoop whispered.

I looked around. "Where are you?" I asked.

"Over here. Behind the big tree," he said.

I looked around for a big tree.

There were a few.

"Which one?" I asked.

"The one that's *talking*!" Snoop snipped.

Hey. I'm sorry. I'm a triplet. From a large family.

I'm used to trying to shut people's voices *out*. Not track them down.

I picked a tree and started walking toward it.

"Not that one, Andrew!" Snoop called.

I headed toward another.

"Not that one, either!" Snoop snapped.

"Oh, for Pete's sake!" I shouted. "Just tell me which one!"

"I'm over *here*," Snoop yelled.

I turned to go toward Snoop. But someone else was behind me.

"So *there* you are!" someone yelled from behind me.

"Andrew, *run*!" Snoop yelled to me.

Not knowing who was behind me, or why I was running, I started to run.

CHAPTER 4

Running seemed like the wisest thing to do at the time.

"So where've you been?" I asked Snoop.

We were running our butts off.

"It's a long story," he replied.

We were side by side.

The chaser, on the other hand, was losing ground with each step we took.

"I think we have time," I noted.

Snoop looked over at me and grinned.

"It's not my fault," he said.

If I'd heard that once, I'd heard it a million times!

"Yeah. Right. It's never your fault," I said as I rolled my eyes.

"Okay. So *sometimes* it's my fault," he admitted grudgingly.

I had to admit, Snoop was being pretty big about this.

Which could only mean one thing.

It really *was* his fault, and he was in the middle of something *huge*!

I wondered if I really wanted to know.

So I asked him.

Failure to Lunch

"Do I even want to *know* what this is about?"

Snoop kept running.

So did I.

The guy was really trailing behind us now.

"If you *do* want to know, you'll have to wait in line," Snoop said. "Behind me."

We turned a corner.

I turned to look at my friend. "What's *that* supposed to mean?!"

"It means I have no idea what's going on," he related.

We turned another corner.

"You must have *some* clue," I argued.

We turned yet another corner.

"Well," he started. "It might have something to do with that bag of money."

That made me stop in my tracks.

"The *what*?!" I shouted.

Snoop stopped running, too.

He looked over his shoulder to see if the guy was still chasing us.

"We must've lost him," Snoop whispered.

"Well, we *did* turn a lot of corners," I whispered back.

"Plus, we were faster than him," Snoop observed.

"Yeah," I snorted a laugh.

"If someone's gonna chase *us*? They'd better be fast!" Snoop remarked.

I was on the track team, and Snoop has always been fast.

But that wasn't the point.

Snoop was smoothing down his shirt.

Not that it needed smoothing or anything. It was just something Snoop did when we was about to show off.

"I don't mean to brag or anything… but…" He kept smoothing. "When you got it? You got it!"

"Yeah," I said. "Well obviously, you got it."

Snoop smiled widely. "Sure 'nuff!"

I wasn't talking about having, you know, the big "it." I was talking about his having someone else's big bag of *money*!

"You're not so bad yourself," Snoop regaled upon me.

I rolled my eyes.

Was he for real?

Here we were, just chased by a big thug, and he's preening like he's all that?

Was he *nuts*?!

If the thug wasn't out of shape? I hated to *think* what would be happening to us right now.

"Would you quit fooling around?!" I barked.

"Who's fooling around?" Snoop asked me.

His big brown eyes were guileless.

He was being serious.

I shook my head. "Snoop. Can we get back to the *problem*?"

"What problem?" he asked. "We got rid of him. Didn't we?"

I sighed loudly. "I'm talking about what you just *told*

me."

"What did I just tell you?" he asked.

"The bag of *money*?!" I shouted.

"Oh yeah. That," he said.

"Are you trying to be this stupid?" I asked him.

He shook his head. "No, man. I just keep trying to forget about it."

We started walking again.

"Well, I don't think you can," I informed him.

He nodded silently.

We headed toward Raul's house. Just in case the thug knew who we were. Or where we lived.

"So tell me the story," I said as calmly as I could.

Snoop nodded his head again.

He looked like a tall, thin bobble head.

"Well, I was headed for gym class," he started.

That, I already knew.

"And I put my backpack down by the door," he went on.

"Okay," I said in support.

I wanted him to know I was still with him.

He nodded again.

"Then I went to take a drink at the water fountain," he stated.

I knew that, too.

"Then I went back to my backpack and picked it up to go into class."

"Okay," I said again.

"But even though it *looked* like my backpack, it didn't feel the same," he said.

I looked at him.

"You know what I mean?" he asked.

"No," I said. "Not really."

He shrugged. "I don't know. It felt different to me."

"Okay," I said. "Whatever. Then what happened?"

"I unzipped the bag and stuck my hand in there."

I didn't know if I'd have done that.

I mean, if it wasn't my backpack, who *knew* what could be in there?!

There could be snakes in there.

Or a scorpion.

Or a person's head or something.

"It was so gross!" he wailed.

See? I *knew* it. It was probably some lopped off head.

"It was prickly, but also hard," he said.

Oh my God! Prickly?

My mind raced.

The only head I knew that was prickly was my Uncle Leopold's.

He was ex-military, but kept the hairstyle.

I shuddered at the image of my Uncle Leopold's severed head.

Sure, he was a pain in the butt. But he didn't deserve to have his head detached. *Or* placed in a backpack.

"What were you just thinking?" Snoop asked me. "You looked all freaked out."

"About my Uncle Leopold's severed head."

Snoop looked disgusted. "You need to stop watching those crime shows, Andrew."

Yeah. Like *that* was going to happen. They were the best shows on TV.

"So what was in the backpack?" I asked, curious.

"Well, when I reached in there and felt the pricklies? It freaked me out. I wasn't expecting that," Snoop explained.

I understood.

"So I dropped the backpack," he said.

I looked at him.

"Well, I kind of threw it down," he clarified.

"Yeah. So?"

"So, when I threw it down? It made a loud cracking noise."

I envisioned a skull cracking on hard pavement.

It wasn't a pretty picture.

Nor was it the most pleasant *sound* one would ever hear.

I imagine it sounded like a cantaloupe smashing.

I pictured bits of that orange stringy stuff globbing out.

And seeds. Slimy seeds.

Thousands of them!

Spread all over the place.

Totally disgusting.

CHAPTER 5

"So what was it?" I asked Snoop.

Snoop started to laugh.

Yeah, that's right. *Laugh!*

Maybe he was losing it.

Maybe he couldn't handle the pressure.

Maybe he was just… nuts.

He finally wound down.

"A Chia pet," he said.

I just looked at him.

"You know," he said. "Ch-ch-ch-*chi*a," he sang.

I kept staring at him.

"It was a *Chia* pet," he said again. "Only it was a little bit dead."

"A dead Chia pet?" I stammered.

"Not all the way dead," he explained. "But almost."

"So let me get this straight," I said. "Someone's chasing us for an almost dead Chia pet?"

That made Snoop laugh.

"No," he said around chuckles. "We're being chased for the *money*."

Okay. So. We were now back to the money.

To be honest, I'd forgotten about it for a minute there.

"When the Chia pet cracked in half, I saw the money," Snoop explained.

That got me thinking.

How much money could someone possibly hide in a Chia pet?!

Probably not much.

Twenty? Fifty? Possibly one hundred dollars?

Surely nothing worth dying for.

Or getting beaten to a pulp over.

"They're all one thousand dollar bills," Snoop supplied.

I was glad he mentioned that little tidbit.

It sort of changed everything.

My outlook.

My level of fear.

Everything.

"Th-th-thousand dollar bills?" I parroted.

"Yeah," he said. "In a Zip-Lock baggie."

"In a Zip-Lock baggie," I repeated softly.

Snoop and I stopped walking.

I just stood there. Trying to soak it all up.

Snoop just stood there. Looking at me.

"How many are there?" I asked.

"Just the one bag," Snoop said.

"I meant the *bills*. How many thousand dollar *bills* are there?" I asked.

I didn't sound like myself. My voice was high-pitched.

I had to be at *least* one octave above my normal tone. (I sounded like Coach Vanoy after he got hit with a hardball in the, ah, peaches.)

"Lots," Snoop said.

I held my breath. "Like, two?" I asked.

"Much more," Snoop answered.

"Five?"

"Nope. Lots more than that," he said seriously.

I let my breath out quickly.

Breathe, Andrew, I reminded myself. *Breathe.*

"I'd say between twenty and thirty," Snoop guessed.

I sucked in my breath quickly! If I hadn't been wearing a belt? My pants would be around my ankles.

"Are you *kidding* me?!" I screamed.

Snoop shook his head. "Nope. Sorry."

I started to choke on my own spit. "You've got to give that money *back*, Snoop!"

"I know. I know!" he shouted back. "Don't you think I tried?!"

"What do you mean you *tried*?" I asked.

He huffed with annoyance.

"I went back to the spot where I left my backpack," he started.

"And?"

"And that big guy was there. He was looking through my backpack," Snoop explained.

"Your *real* backpack?" I asked.

"Yeah," he nodded.

I couldn't believe it! Snoop had had the *perfect* opportunity to return the guy's backpack!

"So why didn't you give his backpack to him *then*?" I demanded.

"Because he was stomping around like a crazy person! He was smashing my backpack against the wall and shouting!"

I thought of all that money.

I'd probably be shouting, too!

"He was saying: 'When I find out who took my backpack, I'm going to KILL them!'"

Okay. So maybe the guy was going postal.

But when he got his money back? He'd probably forget his threat.

I explained that to Snoop.

"You weren't *there*!" he roared. "If you would've *heard* the guy? You'd *know* he would've killed me!"

"So you ran," I said more to myself than to Snoop.

"That's right. It may not sound like it. But at the time? It was the smartest thing to do."

He was right.

It didn't sound like it was the smartest thing to do.

"He knows who I am, man!" Snoop wailed. "My name's on everything in my backpack. Papers, worksheets, books. Danggit! It's even on the waistband of my *gym shorts*!"

"You're fried, my friend," I said sadly.

"I can't go home!" he yowled.

That got me thinking.

"What about your family?!" I said softly.

"Do you think he'll hurt them?" Snoop asked.

"Not if they don't know about the backpack," I guessed.

He nodded.

"And if you think about it. He probably doesn't want too many people knowing about the money," I added.

"Yeah. It can't be legit. Right?" Snoop asked.

"My guess would be no. It's not legitimate."

"Yeah," Snoop agreed. "It *can't* be legal."

It was settled.

The money was most likely dirty.

Right?

I mean, how many kids walk around with twenty or thirty thousand dollars in their backpacks?

Besides this particular one, that is.

Probably—if you count the whole world—I'd say, five to eight kids, tops.

And how many of *them* hide the cash in almost-dead Chia pets?

Using a Zip-Lock baggie.

My guess?

We're down to two or three.

"You're sleeping at my house tonight," I told Snoop.

His face lit up.

I knew what he was thinking. He was thinking about my sister Abbie.

He'd do anything to be near her.

Yes, I know. He's a strange kid.

But I liked him.

It's not *his* fault if he had really bad taste in girls.

He really didn't know Abbie the way I knew her.

Plus, he never seemed annoyed by the things she did. Probably because they were never directed at him. Ever.

In fact, Abbie barely noticed Snoop.

Which was lucky for him.

Take my word.

We hiked over to Raul's house.

I figured I'd call my mom from there to ask if Snoop could stay over.

When we got there, Raul was up in his room.

Probably doing his homework.

Raul was like that. Responsible.

He did his homework as soon as he got home.

Let's just say Snoop and I had a different homework style than Raul.

We waited until the very last minute. Then worked our behinds off to get it done on time.

I guess you could say Snoop and I worked best under pressure.

Or we were lazy.

Take your pick.

We looked in the living room window. He wasn't in there.

And the TV was off.

We circled around to the back of the house and looked in the kitchen window.

Nope. Not there either.

That's why we figured he was up in his room.

We went back to the front door where Snoop stuck his long, skinny finger on the doorbell.

"What a nice surprise," Raul said when he finally came to the door.

"We were leaning on the bell, man," Snoop said.

"What took you so long?!" I grumped.

"I was doing my homework. I was in the middle of a hard math problem," he said.

See? Did I know my friends or what?!

"Look," I said. "I've got to use your phone."

"Yeah," Snoop added. "I switched backpacks by mistake."

"And the new one's got a broken Chia pet in it," I explained.

"Which was stuffed with tons of money," Snoop continued.

"In a Zip-Lock baggie," we said in unison.

We waited for Raul's response.

"Oh," he nodded kind-of blankly.

Then he asked a question.

"What kind of Chia pet?"

CHAPTER 6

Let me get this straight.

We just told him all of that.

And all he wanted to know was... *what kind of Chia pet*?!

"It was a Scooby-Doo," Snoop told Raul.

Raul nodded thoughtfully.

"Scooby-Doo? Or Shaggy?" Raul asked.

"Scooby-Doo," Snoop confirmed.

I shook my head to clear it.

I couldn't believe we were having this conversation.

But then a question popped in my head.

"They make Scooby-Doo and Shaggy Chia pets?"

Snoop and Raul nodded.

"Yup, sure do," Snoop said with grin.

"I think they're limited editions," Raul added. "You only hear about them during the holidays."

"I think there's a reason for that," I muttered to myself.

"Did you know they now have a Shrek Chia pet?" Raul asked Snoop.

"I can go you one *better*!" Snoop replied. "They have a *Donkey* Chia pet."

"No way!" Raul said.

"Sure 'nuff," Snoop said with an important nod.

"Hm," Raul looked impressed. "I did *not* know that."

We moved, as a group, into the living room.

"Now if they'd only make it have Eddie Murphy's *voice*? I'd buy a dozen," Snoop said. "I just *love* Eddie Murphy."

"Yes," Raul agreed. "He's funny."

I stood there with my mouth hanging open.

"Um, guys?" I said. "I hate to interrupt this little Chia pet/Eddie Murphy moment. But can we please get back to the problem?"

Raul and Snoop looked at each other and shared a look.

I chose to ignore what just passed between the two of them.

Mostly because it made me feel a little left out.

I felt that way a lot when my sisters were involved. I didn't like feeling that way with my friends.

I made a mental note.

Note to self. Check out the full line of Chia pets. Including past and present. Everyday and holiday versions. Both regular and limited editions.

There. That should cover it.

"So where's the backpack?" Raul asked as he looked around.

Yeah, I thought. *Where* is *the backpack?!*

"It's at the bus station," Snoop said.

Failure to Lunch

That freaked me out.

"You left a *bag* of *money* at the *bus* station!" I screamed.

Snoop laughed at me.

"Not in the *middle* of the bus station," he said. "What do you take me for? An idiot?"

I let my heart stop tripping.

Snoop laughed. "I left it on the *side* of the bus station."

My heart started tripping again.

I looked at my friend. I pictured what would happen when he couldn't return that money.

"You're going to die," I said to Snoop softly. Sadly.

Snoop just laughed. "I'm just messing with you, Andrew. You're too serious."

I stared at my crazy friend. "You don't think this is serious?"

"Sure, I do," Snoop said. "But I'm not *that* big an idiot."

I hated to ask. "Just *how* big an idiot are you?"

It didn't come out right.

But he got my drift.

"I locked it up in one of those lockers," he said.

Okay. *Now* I could think about my friend not dying.

"Good move," I told Snoop.

Snoop grinned. "I've got *lots* of good moves."

Snoop did his self-named Snoop dance across the living room.

"Like this…" he said as he hopped, skipped, tapped and salsa'd across the room.

I noticed he was headed straight for the kitchen.

"So what now?" Raul asked.

He followed Snoop to the kitchen.

I followed Raul.

"We need to get that backpack," I said.

Snoop headed for the fridge.

"I'm starving. I missed lunch. Mind if I make myself a snack?" he asked Raul.

"Go ahead," Raul said.

"You know," I said. "Now that you brought it up? I was really worried about you at lunch today."

Snoop laughed and looked at Raul.

"He *was* worried," Raul backed me up.

Snoop grinned, then laughed. "You were?"

I watched as he took out jars, bottles, and bags of stuff from Raul's fridge.

"Of course I was!" I barked.

I was annoyed that he'd laughed because I'd worried about him.

"You should have gotten me a message," I yelled.

Snoop went searching through Raul's kitchen cabinets.

"And said what?!" Snoop said with a chuckle.

He put some boxes, cans and sacks on the table.

They sat next to the jars, bottles and stuff from the fridge.

"That I was being hunted down by some giant thug? Who was after his money? Which I found when I broke his Scooby-Doo Chia pet?"

When he put it that way? It did sound a bit... farfetched.

"I was worried about you the whole rest of the day," I told Snoop.

"That's nice," Raul said.

"No, it's not!" I disagreed. "I don't *like* to worry."

I watched as Snoop started building his sandwich.

It was already three inches high and he was still adding to it.

"Well you can stop your worrying," Snoop said. "I'm here. I'm fine. We just have to think about what to do next. Okay?"

He was still piling stuff onto his sandwich. It was now about five and a half inches tall.

"What's that?" I asked. "A Dagwood sandwich?"

"What's a Dagwood sandwich?" Raul asked.

"From the comics. You know. Blondie? Dagwood?" I said.

Raul looked clueless.

"It's a comic strip. Dagwood Bumstead, Blondie's husband, liked to eat big sandwiches," I explained.

Snoop snorted a laugh. "Once, Dagwood's sandwich was so big? It kept falling over. So he drilled a big hole down the middle of it. And then he stuck a frankfurter in the hole to hold it all together."

I saw that Snoop was slopping so much mustard, ketchup and mayo on *his* sandwich, it was holding together like cement.

"Got any salt and pepper?" Snoop asked Raul.

Raul walked over to the kitchen table. He grabbed the two shakers and walked back to Snoop.

"Thanks," Snoop said as he waved the saltshaker over his sandwich.

Then he sprinkled about five shakes of pepper.

"Ah," he said. "Perfect."

The top piece of bread brought the structure to a full six inches.

I waited patiently to see how Snoop would eat it.

I watched. My eyes targeted and ready.

And then it happened.

It looked like a snake adjusting its lower jaw to suck down a rat.

I watched as Snoop's mouth opened wide enough to take in a six-inch-tall sandwich.

It was both fascinating and disgusting at the same time.

"Some people thought Dagwood was an idiot," Snoop mentioned through his mouthful of triple-decker.

Raul and I just kept staring.

"But I thought he was a genius," Snoop concluded.

CHAPTER 7

Raul went back to his room to finish his homework.

And I had the pleasure of watching Snoop finish his sandwich.

As soon as Snoop was done, I called for Raul.

"Come on. We've got to go!" I shouted up the stairs.

"Wait a minute," he called back. "I only have a couple more questions to go."

"We've got to go *now*!" I urged. "Before it gets too late."

"I just want to finish this first. Get it all done," Raul called back. "In case something goes wrong while we're out."

Snoop snorted a laugh. "I don't know about you," he said to me. "But I'm thinking that if something goes wrong while we're out? We're not going to *be* at school tomorrow."

I wasn't thinking that at all. Instead, I was thinking about my quote from English class.

The man who goes alone can start today. But he who travels with another must wait till that other is ready.

Henry David Thoreau *really* knew what he was talking about.

He probably had friends like mine. You know, dawdlers!

That's what my mom called us when any of us lagged behind or did something slowly. Dawdlers.

So we waited. And waited.

Snoop walked back to Raul's living room and turned on the TV. He plopped into one of the big comfy chairs.

I took the couch.

"Nothing's on," Snoop complained.

"Just news," I noticed.

So Snoop kept flipping through the channels.

He was flipping so fast, I couldn't catch a thing.

Plus, I felt like I was going to have a seizure from all the flashing pictures.

"Would you knock it off?!" I said to Snoop.

"It's just news," he said.

"So either *pick* a channel, or turn it off," I said.

The TV had stopped on a local news show.

"Hey, I know that guy," I said aloud. "He's one of the reporters I met!"

"From the bank heist?" Snoop asked me.

"Yeah."

The reporter always looked the same.

Big, plastic smile. Lots of white teeth. And that hair.

"Is that a rug?" Snoop asked me.

"One of the blond women from another channel said it was," I answered.

"It sort of looks like it is," Snoop said.

He was squinting at the TV screen. Inspecting.

"But maybe it's not," he concluded. "It *could* be real. It's just too… perfect."

Personally? I couldn't give a, um, poop.

"Does it make a difference?" I said with annoyance.

Snoop got up and walked over to the TV.

His face was three inches away from the screen.

"I don't know. I just can't tell," he muttered.

Just then, Raul's mom came through the door.

"Hi boys," she said cheerfully.

Then she caught sight of the TV.

"Oh, turn that up, please," she said.

She put her briefcase on the coffee table. Then she kicked off her shoes. Then she sat down on one of the big comfy chairs.

"The silent auction is said to be bringing in quite the sum," the plastic-smiled guy said smoothly.

There were lots of things on tables around him.

"Hey," Snoop said. "Isn't that our school gym?"

Raul's mom smiled. "Yes it is."

Snoop turned pale. Well, as pale as Snoop could turn.

He was worried! And I knew why.

What if they were reporting on the "stolen" money?

The money that Snoop mistakenly stole?!

All eyes were plastered on the TV.

"This is great," Raul's mom said happily.

Great?! Was she kidding?!

"We wanted more people involved in the school

district fundraiser," she said to us.

We just stared at her.

"I'm on the committee," she added.

We still stared.

"This year, the fund drive didn't bring in *nearly* as much as former years," she said.

"Why not?" I asked.

"We have no idea. The cash jars weren't enough. Although they usually were."

"Cash jars?" Snoop asked.

"At the schools, around town," she explained.

"Those big glass jars," I told Snoop.

Raul's Mom nodded. "Yes, well, we had to do more fundraising to meet our goal this year."

She looked at the TV.

"We came up with the silent auction. We're hoping to get more people contributing," she explained.

We turned back to the TV.

"And over here, we have a romantic dinner for two at Chez Henri," the reporter said. "The opening bid is fifty dollars."

The reporter read a piece of paper.

"It's a five course meal, folks," he said with another plastic smile.

"Ewww," Raul's mother said. "I think I'll bid on that. Excuse me."

She got up, reached into her briefcase, and took out her cell phone.

"Don't tell Raul's dad," she said to us. "Okay?"

I looked at Snoop. He shrugged.

"Sure," we said together.

She left the room with her cell phone smashed to her ear.

I looked back to the TV set. The reporter had moved on to another item. It looked like a basket of wrinkle creams or something. Nothing exciting.

We shut off the TV.

"Let's see if Raul's done," I suggested.

We clomped up to his room. He was still working.

"What's going on?" Snoop demanded.

"I thought you only had a couple more problems to do?" I asked.

Raul made a face. "They're a lot harder than I thought. It's taking me longer than I figured."

"So when will you be done?" Snoop asked.

Raul looked upset. "Not any time soon."

"So let's go now," Snoop said.

Raul hesitated.

"Hi, honey," Raul's mom said as she joined us in Raul's room. "How was your day?"

"Good," he said. "And yours?"

She shrugged. "Busy, but good."

He nodded. "Can I go out with Andrew and Snoop for a little while?"

"Is your homework done?" she asked Raul.

"Not yet," he said.

She made a face.

We all knew what *that* face meant. All of our mothers had their own version of that face.

"Don't sweat it," Snoop said to Raul. "We can go another time."

I looked at Snoop.

He shrugged. "We'd better head home, anyhow. Your mom'll be mad if we're not home for dinner."

I looked at the clock next to Raul's bed. 5:18.

Wow. When had it gotten so late?

"Yeah," I said. "We'd better go."

So Snoop and I left Raul's house.

"What are we going to do now?" I asked Snoop.

We were walking home to my house. Snoop couldn't go home. You know, in case the thug was waiting for him.

"The backpack will still be in the locker tomorrow," Snoop said with a shrug.

"What about school?" I asked him.

"Oh, yeah," he said. His shoulders hung low. "Guess I can't go until this is settled."

"What are you going to do tomorrow? During the day?" I asked.

"I'll think of something," he said with a slow smile.

When we got home, my mom said that Snoop could stay over.

We told her that we were working on a project. Which was kind of true.

CHAPTER 8

The next day was weird.

I was having trouble keeping my mind on school stuff. I was too worried about Snoop.

I wondered where he was.

I wondered what he was doing.

I wondered if he was keeping out of trouble.

As you can tell, he had an uncanny way of finding trouble.

He was like a pig finding truffles.

No one knew *how* they did it. But they did.

And so did Snoop. Find trouble, that is. Not truffles.

I don't really even know what truffles actually are.

Some sort of fungus or something.

Anyhow, I was sitting in English class. Trying to listen and not think about Snoop. When all of a sudden, Vice Principal Truman barged in.

He stood in front of the class and pointed to Tyrone. "*You*! Come with me!"

Tyrone looked up at him with heavy lids.

"What for?" Tyrone asked.

"Just do as you're told!" the vice principal barked.

No one liked Vice Principal Truman. He was a real

idiot.

Thought he was all that.

But he wasn't.

He was just a jerk. And everyone but him knew it.

Tyrone looked at Ms. Gold.

She made a face. "I guess you should go," she said to Tyrone.

Tyrone got up slowly.

I'm sure he did it to tick off Mr. Truman.

It worked.

Truman was out of patience. "Move it, slug!" he roared.

Tyrone slowly dragged his way up to Vice Principal Truman.

Truman took four giant steps to the door. He pulled it open with way too much force, and then waited.

Tyrone inched his way across the room.

"And pull up your pants!" Truman yelled at Tyrone.

Tyrone just latched onto his pants and shifted them around a bit. But they still hung low.

It was his style. His look.

And I doubted Vice Principal Truman was going to change it any time soon.

Not without Tyrone *wanting* it to change.

Tyrone edged through the doorway. Oh so slowly.

It was pretty funny to watch. (And mind you, we were *all* watching.)

I could see Tyrone's face through the little window on

the door.

He was shaking his head.

He was shrugging.

Then, I could swear he was saying, "Not me." (*If* I was reading his lips correctly.)

Tyrone kept saying that over and over.

I shifted in my seat a little bit so I could get a glimpse of Mr. Truman.

His face was red and he was swinging his arms all over the place.

He looked like he wanted to kill Tyrone.

Then, suddenly, Vice Principal Truman swung open the door.

"Did you kick Tyrone out of class yesterday?" he shouted at Ms. Gold.

"No," she said.

"You didn't send him to the principal's office?" he demanded loudly.

"No."

"He was in your class the *entire* period?" he roared.

"Yes," Ms. Gold said. "He didn't even leave to use the restroom."

"You're sure?!" he barked.

"Positive," she said sweetly. A little too sweetly.

That made Tyrone smile.

It also made Mr. Truman stalk out of the room angrily.

The room was silent.

No one knew what to say or do.

Finally, Tyrone sounded off. "What was up with *that*?!"

Ms. Gold shrugged. "I have *no* idea."

"What'd you *do* to the man, Tyrone?" someone asked from the back of the room.

"I didn't do anything!" Tyrone said in his defense.

"Well what did he want?" Ms Gold asked.

Tyrone shrugged. "The guy's a freak! He was all over me. For no reason!"

Tyrone walked back to his seat.

"He's such a jerk," someone said aloud.

"Okay," Ms. Gold said. "Let's just get back to work. All right?"

It wasn't all right with Tyrone. At least, not yet.

He was still upset.

"That man's gone and lost his mind!" Tyrone muttered softly to himself.

"Turn your books to page two forty-six, everyone," Ms. Gold called out.

I turned to page two forty-six.

Tyrone was still talking to himself quietly.

"Giving me grief about some stupid Chia pet!" he muttered so only I could hear.

What?! Did he just say: Chia pet?

I turned to Tyrone. "He was asking you about a Chia pet?"

Tyrone looked at me.

"Now what would *I* want with some stupid Chia pet?!" he whispered to me.

"I don't know," I squeaked.

I sounded like I'd just sucked down some helium.

"He says I stole it from the principal's office yesterday!" Tyrone fumed as quietly as he could.

Tyrone looked at me head on.

"Yesterday, I wasn't even *in* the principal's office," he said a little too loudly.

Ms. Gold stopped talking. "Is there a problem back there, boys?"

"No," I eked out.

Everyone laughed at my high-pitched response.

But I didn't care about that. I had other, more important things to worry about.

Like, why was Mr. Truman looking for the Chia pet?

And if it was from the principal's office? Why wasn't Mrs. Caldor—the principal—looking for it?

That was odd.

Something was weird about all this.

"Me!" Tyrone muttered quietly. "A *Chia* pet!"

I looked over at Tyrone.

"Why would *I* want a Chia pet?! They're *definitely* not cool!" he added.

Yeah, I thought. *Tell Snoop and Raul that, would ya?*

"And blaming a brotha every time there's a problem?! That's definitely not cool, either!" Tyrone huffed.

"Tyrone?" Ms. Gold said. "Is there something you'd

like to share with the class?"

Tyrone was getting himself all worked up.

"Yeah," he said tightly. "I think Truman needs to freshen up on the quotes of Henry David Thoreau! That's all I'm sayin'."

We all remembered the quote Tyrone had picked yesterday. The one about how it's never too late to give up your prejudices.

Wow. This Thoreau guy was more on the mark than I thought! And I thought he was pretty on the mark *before* all this happened.

I could barely wait for lunch. I needed to tell Raul about this latest twist.

Maybe he could figure out what was going on!

Because *I* couldn't!

CHAPTER 9

"So let me get this straight," Raul said.

He went right to his dessert since Tater-Tots weren't served today.

"Mr. Truman was looking for the Chia pet?" he asked me.

"Right," I said.

"But it was taken from Mrs. *Caldor's* office?" Raul asked.

"That's right," I confirmed.

"Well, why isn't Mrs. Caldor looking for it?" he asked me.

I nodded. "That's what I was thinking."

Raul studied his giant cookie.

He took a bite.

Then he took a swig of his chocolate milk.

"Maybe Mrs. Caldor doesn't know it's *missing*," Raul said slowly.

"I wonder if she knew about the money inside it?" I said aloud.

I wasn't really asking Raul a question. The thought just popped into my head.

"That's an even *better* question," Raul mused.

We sat there eating our lunches. Without Snoop.

I liked Raul and all, but it was kind of lonely.

"Isn't your mom friends with Mrs. Caldor's assistant?" Raul asked me.

"You mean, Mrs. Franks? Yeah. Why?"

"Because she'd know about the Chia pet/money problem," he said. "Right?"

If anyone would know? She'd know.

"Come on," I said to Raul. "Let's go visit her."

Raul didn't look too keen on the idea.

"What if Mrs. Caldor's there?" he asked me.

"Well," I said. "It *is* her office. So there's always that chance."

Our principal, Mrs. Caldor, really creeped out Raul.

But I think he'd be creeped out by *any* principal.

Raul was a good kid. Did things by the book.

He went out of his way to stay out of trouble.

But sometimes? You had to dance near the devil, so to speak.

This was one of those times.

We needed to see Mrs. Caldor's assistant, and I wanted Raul there with me.

Just in case I forgot to ask a vital question.

I figured we only had one shot to get the info we needed.

More than one casual inquiry? And *we'd* be suspects.

"Don't worry, Raul. Mrs. Caldor probably won't come out to where Mrs. Franks sits," I said.

"Are you sure?" he asked.

Failure to Lunch

His swarthy Latino skin looked a little pale. And a gleam of sweat showed on his forehead.

"Don't sweat it, Raul," I said. "Literally."

He didn't look assured.

I spoke quickly. "Mrs. Caldor rarely leaves her office. If she wants to speak with Mrs. Franks? She buzzes her. Has Mrs. Franks come into *her* office."

It sounded good to me.

I had no idea if it was true or not. But it sounded good to me.

It must've sounded good to Raul too.

"Okay," he said. "Let's go."

We left the lunchroom and walked to the principal's office.

"What if we get caught in the hallway without a pass?" Raul asked me.

"We're going to the *principal's* office," I said. "What can anyone do to us?"

Raul laughed nervously. "Yes. That's true. We're already headed to where they'd send us."

We got there in about two minutes.

"Hi, boys," Mrs. Franks said. "How may I help you?"

You know? I probably should've put a little thought into how I was going to *start* this conversation.

I had nothing.

I panicked.

I looked at Raul.

He was sweating up a storm.

The perfect storm.

It looked like he had a tidal wave on his forehead.

The guy had, like, a tsunami of sweat rolling across his brow.

It was up to me.

"Mrs. Franks?" I asked.

"Yes, Andrew?"

It was now or never.

I had to go on automatic pilot.

That meant: open mouth and hope the brain was in gear.

"Is there, by any chance, anything missing from Mrs. Caldor's office?" I asked softly.

Mrs. Franks got up and walked to the principal's door.

"No, wait!" Raul shouted.

The tsunami was dripping down his cheeks.

A sweat drop blobbed off his nose.

It was *huge*!

The sweat drop. Not Raul's nose.

Well, now that I was mentioning it? His nose *was* a little large. But not, you know, huge.

"It's okay," Mrs. Franks said. "Mrs. Caldor's out at a meeting. We can go and look if you'd like."

She opened up the door.

The door to Principal Caldor's office.

The door behind which Raul never wanted to be.

He looked terrified.

Me? I'd been in there before.

A few times.

Sure, they weren't the most *pleasant* experiences I've ever had.

But they sure weren't the worst experiences, either.

"Come along," Mrs. Franks said to Raul and me.

She flipped on the light.

"So how's it look?" I asked Mrs. Franks.

She looked around.

"The same as always," she said.

"Anything missing?" Raul asked.

She looked around again.

"Not that I can tell," she said easily.

Over in the far corner, there was a bookcase.

But instead if books, it held a whole bunch of doo-dads and stuff.

"What's that?" I asked Mrs. Franks.

She laughed.

Then she coughed into her hand a little.

"It's where Mrs. Caldor puts all the gifts she receives from students."

"There aren't too many," Raul observed.

"And they're all junk," I noted.

Mrs. Franks laughed and coughed into her hand again.

She looked around quickly. Then she lowered her voice to a whisper.

"I refer to that area as..." she looked around again. "The gift graveyard shelves."

Raul and I walked over to the shelves.

They were crowded with lots of stupid things.

You know, like little ceramic figurines and tiny trophies and stuff.

They were also covered with dust.

Obviously they've been sitting there for a while.

"Hey," Raul said as he leaned over one of the bottom shelves. "Look at this."

I knelt to look.

There was a big empty spot.

And it didn't have dust in the center.

Mrs. Franks came to look, too.

"Something was here," Raul said.

"And now it's not," I added.

"Do you recall what it was?" Raul asked Mrs. Franks.

She shook her head. "I have no idea. Just some little knick-knack, I'm sure. Nothing of value."

Yeah. That's what *she* thought.

CHAPTER 10

The bell rang. Our lunch period was over.

We thanked Mrs. Franks and then left.

"What do you think?" I asked Raul.

"I think we need to find the kid who stole the Chia pet," he answered.

"How are we going to do that?" I asked.

Raul sighed heavily. "I think we need to bring Snoop back to school."

"But he'll get killed!" I argued.

"Not if he returns the money to the guy who's after him," Raul noted.

"But…" a thought was forming in my head. But not quickly enough.

We kept walking to our lockers.

"But what if Vice Principal Truman goes after Snoop?" I finally said.

Raul shook his head.

"No. Snoop said that some big kid was after the backpack. Remember?" Raul asked me.

"Yeah. So?"

"So if we can protect Snoop *from* that kid. And return the money *to* that kid. There will *be* no problem," Raul explained.

"But what about Truman?" I asked.

"As long as Snoop doesn't have the money? He's not Snoop's problem. Truman is the *other* kid's problem."

Raul was right. That made sense.

"Okay, so now what?" I asked.

"We finish the day, today," Raul said. "Tomorrow, Snoop returns to school."

"We'll have to hang by his side during his gym period, though. Don't you think?" I asked Raul.

"I don't think I'm going to be much help," Raul said softly.

I knew he didn't want to be there. He was scared.

But he was also right.

He really wouldn't be much help.

So it was just Snoop and me. Together.

Returning the thug's backpack. *With* the Scooby-Doo Chia pet. *And* the wad of money in the Zip-Lock baggie.

I figured the big bully would be happy to get it back. So maybe he *wouldn't* kill us.

But I was just guessing.

I had plenty of time to worry about it. The day dragged on forever.

Finally, the bell rang and it was time to go home.

I figured Snoop would find me again today like he did yesterday.

Only today? My sisters were walking home from the bus *with* me.

Wasn't I lucky.

And to make things worse? I could hear them talking.

"In homeroom, we had on the Today show," Abbie said to Annie.

"It's not the same without Katie Couric," Annie commented.

"True," Abbie said. "Anyhow. They had on Fabio."

Annie made a face. "You *like* him?"

It was Abbie's turn to make a face. "Ugh. *No*! But he said something *so* funny!"

I couldn't believe my ears.

Here, one of my best friends was barely escaping death. He came across *thousands* of dollars, by *mistake*. And tomorrow? Who *knew* what would happen to him?!

And they're talking about *Fabio*?

"What did he say?" Annie asked Abbie.

Abbie laughed. "He didn't know what a chicken potpie was."

"You're kidding!" Annie gasped.

"I *know*!" Abbie gushed. "How weird is *that*?!"

"In this day and age," Annie commented. "*Very* weird."

The conversation wasn't over yet.

They went on and on and on about Fabio. And about his never having a chicken potpie. And about how weird it all was.

It was torture to listen to! Complete torture.

I was almost ready to kill myself.

But then Snoop showed up.

"Hey, Leeg family," Snoop said smoothly as he slid next to Abbie.

Abbie and Annie were still beating the Fabio/chicken potpie topic like a dead horse. So they didn't respond.

Snoop looked disappointed.

He slowed down a pace or two and got in step with me.

"How was your day?" I asked him.

He shrugged. "Better than school, I'm sure. How was yours?"

"Interesting," I said.

We kept walking toward home.

Snoop was watching Abbie, but she had no clue.

If you can believe it, they were *still* talking about Fabio and chicken potpie.

I sighed. "Girls."

Snoop grinned. "Can't live with 'em. Can't live without 'em."

I begged to differ. But we had more important things to discuss.

"Something weird happened in English class today," I said.

I told him about the vice principal.

"Then Raul and I visited the principal's office," I added.

"On your *own*?" he shrieked. "Without being called *down*?!"

Failure to Lunch

"Well, yeah. We needed to check things out."

"Like what?" he asked.

"Like where the Chia pet came from," I explained.

He was finally getting it.

"Oh, right," he said. "Was anything *else* missing?"

"I think it was the only thing missing from the gift graveyard shelf."

"The what?" Snoop asked.

"The gift graveyard shelf. It's where Mrs. Caldor puts her gifts from parents and students and stuff."

Snoop made a face. "She gets *gifts*?!"

I shrugged. "I guess so. But not too many. And they're all pretty dumb."

Snoop nodded.

"So how'd you know nothing else was missing?" Annie asked me.

I was so into my tale, I didn't notice that my sisters were listening. Great. Just great!

"Ewwww," Abbie said. "There's major drama going on at school!"

Snoop stuck his thumb at his chest. "And *I'm* the star."

I rolled my eyes.

God, he'd do *anything* to get her attention!

It was disgusting.

"There was only one spot where there was an empty dust hole." I told Annie.

She nodded. "Was there dust on every shelf?"

69

Elise Leonard

"Yes," I replied.

"So nothing else was moved," she said.

"But why is Mr. Truman all nuts about it?" Abbie asked.

Snoop fielded that question. "He must have something to do with the money."

I belted Snoop across his chest.

Was he nuts?! Blurting it out like that?!

The less people who knew, the better!

Especially *these* two yackbirds!

Before long, *everyone* would know about this whole mess!

"What money?" Abbie asked Snoop.

He looked at me.

His eyes said, "I *know* I shouldn't tell her." But his mouth said, "The twenty-seven thousand dollars."

Abbie's eyes flew open in surprise.

Annie gasped.

"Oh, my God!" Abbie muttered.

"How'd you guys get caught up in this?" Annie asked Snoop and me.

I pointed to Snoop.

That was all I had to say.

"Truman's a jerk!" Abbie spit out with emotion.

"I think he's connected to the money," I said.

"And I think we need to prove it," Annie added.

"Maybe we can get him fired," Abbie finished.

Snoop whooped with joy. "We'll be heroes!"

CHAPTER 11

"Okay. You take Truman," Abbie said to Annie.

"Hey," I said. "Wait a minute!"

Abbie looked at me and made a face.

"Who made *you* the boss?" I said to her.

"I did," she said simply. "I'm the smartest one here."

"Says who?" I argued.

"Says me," Abbie hurled back.

I looked around quickly for effect. "*Annie's* smarter than you."

Abbie shrugged. "Maybe. But she doesn't have the guts."

Annie looked offended. "The guts?"

"To do what it takes," Abbie explained.

Annie thought about that for a moment. Then she shrugged. "You're probably right."

I was insulted. "What about *me*?" I asked loudly.

Abbie rolled her eyes and laughed. "You're kidding. Right?"

"No!" I shouted. "I'm *not* kidding!"

She looked at me, her face contorting into an evil grin. "Andy-boy, you're just not a good leader."

Grrr. I *hated* when she called me Andy-boy.

"The name's Andrew," I said. "And I *am* a good leader."

"No you're not," Abbie said.

"Yes I am," I said.

"Are not," she said.

"Am, too!"

"Are not."

"Am, too!"

Okay. So at the moment, we *both* sounded like three year olds. But she made me so angry!

"Look," Snoop said to the two of us. "This isn't getting us anywhere."

"Yeah," I agreed.

"So what do *you* suggest we do?" Abbie asked Snoop.

"I don't know. But why do we have to involve Truman?" Snoop asked.

"Because he's all bent out of shape," Annie said.

"Over a Chia pet," Abbie added.

"With twenty-seven thousand dollars in it!" Annie finished.

"What if we just return the backpack to the kid?" Snoop suggested.

"Yeah," I seconded. "Then this whole mess won't be our problem."

"It'll be the kid's problem," Snoop explained.

The girls stared at us.

"Don't you want to know where that money's coming from?" Annie asked Snoop and me.

"Not really," I said.

I looked at Snoop.

He shrugged.

"And don't you want to know why it was hidden in Mrs. *Caldor's* office but Mr. *Truman* is looking for it?" Abbie asked.

That *did* have me curious. Plus the whole "getting Truman fired" thing was cool.

"All right," I said. "We'll do it your way."

"So what do we do, boss?" Snoop asked Abbie.

I looked at Snoop.

He was all staring at Abbie and grinning like an idiot.

The guy was an imbecile. He'd do *anything* to get her attention. It was pathetic!

"Annie will take Truman," she said to Annie.

Annie nodded. "I'll be discreet."

"Find out what he's doing that might give him the opportunity to get his hands on that kind of money."

"It may be the silent auction," I mentioned.

Everyone stared at me.

"The what?" Abbie asked.

"The school district. It's trying to drum up money. So they're having a silent auction," I said.

"On donated stuff," Snoop added.

Abbie looked at Annie.

"There's his opportunity," Annie said.

Abbie nodded. "Yeah. So keep an eye on him. And watch that auction."

Hah! Good leader my butt!

"She can't watch the silent auction," I told Abbie. "It's a *silent* auction!"

Abbie looked annoyed. "What does that mean?"

"It means that people see the stuff on TV," I explained. "Then they call in their bid."

"Who's taking those calls?" Annie asked.

"I don't know. My guess?" I said. "Truman."

"Okay," Abbie said to Annie. "Find out about that."

"When is the auction on the TV?" Annie asked me.

"Late afternoons. On the news," I said.

"On the station with the guy with the plastic hair," Snoop added.

Annie smiled. "Okay. I'll watch."

Abbie turned to Snoop. "You need to question the guy with the backpack."

"Why me?" Snoop asked.

"Because you know who he is!" she said in frustration.

"I think we should go together to question him," I said.

"Why?" Annie asked.

"So Snoop doesn't get hurt," I explained. "The guy's a big bully."

"And the last time I saw him?" Snoop said. "He was *really* ticked off."

"He's probably in on it with Truman," Abbie muttered to herself.

"Yeah," I said. "But you know what Dad always says. We need to build a solid case."

Annie agreed with me.

And that convinced Abbie.

"Okay," Abbie said. "Let's question him together. When and where?"

She looked at Snoop.

"Tomorrow. By the water fountain in front of the gym. Before third period," Snoop said.

It was set.

CHAPTER 12

We got there early.

Snoop, Abbie, Annie and I waited for the big kid.

When he arrived, Snoop pointed him out.

"That really big kid?" Annie asked. She swallowed hard.

"Yup," Snoop said. "That's the one."

"He's a senior," Abbie commented.

"You know him?" I asked my sister.

She shook her head. "No. But I've heard about him."

Great. His reputation preceded him.

We were going to get our butts kicked by a big, angry senior.

This'll look just great on my school resume.

Abbie started walking toward the big brute.

"Yo," she said to him.

He turned and eyed her.

"What?" he asked.

"We want to talk to you," she said boldly.

But then she noticed that she was standing alone.

She turned around and signaled to us.

Her signal said, "Get your scaredy-butts over here *right* now! Or *I'll* give you something to be afraid of!"

It was a very effective signal.

We all ran over to her.

True, we were cowering. But I was hoping he couldn't tell that we were mostly chickenhearted. I mean, we *did* outnumber him.

Four to one.

But even at those odds? He could take us easily.

Except for possibly one thing.

We had Abbie.

And when Abbie got mad?

She was like fifteen people.

And sadly for him? He was about to make Abbie mad.

"What do you idiots want?!" he bellowed. "I don't have time for little kids!"

I could see the switch turn on.

He'd just pressed the red button.

You know the one.

The big red button? The one your fingers *itch* to press?

The one with the sign that says: **For emergency only!**

The one where there's always someone standing nearby.

And they're usually saying, "Whatever you do, *don't* press that red button!"

Well, this big, blundering egomaniac went and did it.

He pressed the big red button!

And now, he'd better look out.

"Look, buster," Abbie said to the guy. "We *said* we

need to talk with you."

His eyes widened slightly.

Apparently, not many people speak to him that way.

I know *I* wouldn't!

"We found something that belongs to you," she continued. "And unless you don't want it back, you'd better answer a few questions!"

Wow. She was *awesome*!

She was poking that guy in his chest like he was the Pillsbury doughboy.

I almost expected to hear that silly giggle.

You know, the one the Pillsbury doughboy makes?

But he sure wasn't giggling.

I waited for him to get mad.

Really mad.

I know if *I'd* been the one poking him like that? He'd be furious by now.

But instead of getting mad? He looked worried.

Really worried.

But then I thought about it a little. And realized that yeah, he *should* be worried!

When Abbie got this ticked off? It was every man for himself!

"Sure," he said angrily. "I'll answer your questions."

"Good," Abbie said.

She grabbed his shirt and twisted.

Now I didn't know too much about the anatomy of seniors. But by looking at his hairy arms? I'd guess

Failure to Lunch

Abbie had a few chest hairs caught up in her fist.

She twisted again.

Harder.

His anger seemed to fade quickly.

And sweat was beading up on his forehead.

I looked at Snoop.

He was staring at Abbie and grinning widely.

Then I looked at Annie.

She looked like she was going to throw up.

"So tell me about the items in your backpack," Abbie said quietly.

I was glad she wasn't spouting off about the money too loudly.

We didn't need to attract a bigger crowd than we'd already drawn.

And we didn't need people jumping Snoop for the backpack he was holding.

Who knew what twenty-seven thousand in cash would do to people.

A riot could break out. And there'd be no way to stop it.

"Look," the kid said. "Just give me the backpack back. Yours is in my locker. I'll go get it."

"Not so fast," Abbie said, and twisted again.

I think the guy whimpered.

"What do you want?" he asked.

"We want to know what's up with the Chia pet," Abbie said.

The guy turned gray.

He said nothing.

"Answer the question!" Abbie hollered.

She twisted his shirt again.

Still no answer.

"Perhaps we should involve Mr. Truman," Abbie said.

"Or Mrs. Caldor," I added.

"Or the police," Annie finished.

The senior was looking around nervously.

Sweat was pouring from his brow now.

"Okay, okay," he finally whispered. "I'll tell you. Just keep your voices down."

I was certain he was trying not to incite a money-lusting riot.

We all crowded around him.

Packed so close, I could feel the heat coming from his body.

I could smell his fear.

Or maybe it was just BO.

"All right," he said softly. "I stole it."

"Why?" Annie asked him.

He looked at her.

His eyes begged her not to ask that question.

But that was Annie. She wanted to know. *Had* to know the truth.

He looked around.

He motioned for us to come closer.

I didn't see how that could be done.

Failure to Lunch

We were all squooshed together already.

The last time I was this squooshed was when I was on a crowded subway in NYC at rush hour.

"I took it because I've always wanted a Chia pet," he whispered softly.

We all stared at him.

I couldn't speak for anyone else, but I was expecting more.

"And it was *Scooby-Doo*," he added.

We kept staring.

"I used to love Scooby-Doo as a kid," he tried to explain.

We were still staring.

"Look," he said. "I have a reputation to uphold."

Abbie made a face. "As what? A bully?"

He looked embarrassed. "Yeah. Kinda."

"So what does that have to do with any of *this*?" I asked him.

He looked at me. His eyes pleading.

"Don't make me explain," he said in a tortured voice.

You know, if we'd beaten him up, I don't think it would've been more painful for him.

All these questions seemed to be the greatest torture we could bring to him.

"Sorry, but you'll have to explain," Abbie said.

She was relentless.

She had her man and she was showing no mercy.

Maybe the big bully would think about that the next

time *he* was tormenting someone.

He sighed heavily.

He was about to confess.

I saw Abbie loosen her hold on his shirt. Slightly.

"I've always wanted a Chia pet," he started. "But I'd never *buy* one! What if someone saw it getting delivered?!"

We waited for more.

"I couldn't *ask* for one," he explained. "You know, as a gift."

"*And*?" Abbie said snottily.

"And I couldn't admit to even *wanting* one!" he squeaked.

"Why not?" Annie asked him.

"Because it would hurt my *image*!"

I wouldn't admit it to anyone, but I kind of agreed with the guy.

"I mean," he tried to explain. "Can you picture *the Rock* with a Chia pet?"

Abbie broke out laughing. "You equate yourself with the Rock?"

The guy looked insulted. "Well, yeah."

"Then you'd better start working out," she told him boldly. "Right now you're more like the Hamburger Bun than the Rock."

He looked totally insulted.

But that was Abbie.

She could really bring you down about yourself.

And she did it so easily, too.

Take my word.

Been there, done that.

I was busy thinking about all the times Abbie had made me feel like dirt.

Too busy to notice that the bully was crying.

"Look," he said. "I don't want it getting out that I wanted a Chia pet. I'll be laughed out of school."

"Oh, I'm telling!" Abbie said. "I'm telling *everyone*!"

He started to sob.

It was really pathetic.

"But it was Scooby-Doo," he said. "And it was dying. I couldn't let it sit there on the shelf and just die."

The guy was blubbering like a two-year-old. It was pitiful.

I couldn't take it.

I had to do something.

"Okay, okay," I said. "We won't tell anyone."

"We won't?" Abbie asked.

"No. We won't," I stated firmly.

"Thank you," the guy said through little hiccupping sobs.

"But only if you tell us about the money," I added.

CHAPTER 13

The bell rang and the crowd broke up.

It was just him and us now.

Plus, since there wasn't a fight? Everyone got bored and walked away anyhow.

So no one had heard the part about the money.

"What money?" the kid asked.

"The money in the Chia pet," Snoop said.

The kid looked confused.

"There was money in the Chia pet?" he asked.

We all looked at each other.

Could this be true?

Did he *not* know about the money?

Could he not know about the money?

"Why were you going ballistic about the switched backpacks?" I asked him.

He looked at me. "Because I didn't want anyone finding out that I wanted—or had—a Chia pet!"

"That's it?" Snoop asked him.

"Yeah," he said. "Why?"

"Because you looked totally freaked out when I went to give you back your backpack," Snoop said.

"I told you. My *rep* was at stake," he said.

"And now your *butt's* at stake!" Snoop told him.

"Why? Because I stole it from the principal?" he asked.

"No," Snoop said. "Because it was filled with money!"

"It was?" he asked.

"*Lots* of money!" I said.

He didn't seem to care about the money.

I say that because of what he said next.

"No *wonder* the poor thing was dying," he said.

"So now what do we do?" Snoop asked.

"I think we'd better go to Mrs. Caldor," Annie said.

"Don't we have any other options?" the bully asked.

"You don't have a vote here," Snoop told him.

Just then, Vice Principal Truman came storming over.

He pointed at Snoop. "What are *you* doing here?!" he yelled.

That threw me off a little.

I mean, we were *all* late for class. We were *all* standing together.

But Truman had only picked on Snoop.

I remembered what Tyrone had said about Mr. Truman blaming a "brotha" every time there was a problem.

And all of a sudden, *I* was really angry.

"We were all cutting class," I said. "Got a *problem* with that?"

Abbie laughed.

85

Annie gasped.

Snoop looked like he'd just seen his dead great-grandmother.

And the senior just stood there quietly.

"That's it," Truman shouted. "I'm hauling you kids down to the office. Starting with *you*," he said to Snoop.

Snoop just kept staring at Mr. Truman.

"Move it, *maggots*!" Truman yelled.

We turned and started walking to the main office.

But that wasn't good enough for Truman. No.

He started *shoving* Snoop.

"Keep your hands off our friend, you jerk!" Abbie said to the vice principal.

Snoop was so happy Abbie had called him her "friend," that he wasn't as insulted as he should've been.

And that only got me *more* riled up.

"Yeah, you big Neanderthal!" I said. "Quit shoving!"

Truman made the stupid mistake of shoving Snoop again.

Abbie and I went *completely* ballistic!

We were almost at the office by now.

Within earshot—*if* we were very loud.

Mrs. Caldor's private office was right behind that nearby door.

It was an exit for her office. But locked from the outside. So you couldn't go in from there. Only out.

If you wanted to go in? You had to go through Mrs. Franks' area. By the school's front door.

But Mrs. Caldor's private office was right behind that door.

And we all knew that.

"I want to speak with the principal!" Annie shouted loudly.

"I want to speak with a lawyer!" Abbie said, equally loudly.

"I want to speak with the police!" I commanded as loudly as I could.

We knew the ruckus would bring out Mrs. Caldor.

And as expected, she bustled right out her private door.

Mrs. Caldor did that. She "bustled."

"What is going on out here?!" she demanded.

"They're cutting class," Mr. Truman told Mrs. Caldor.

She looked at all of us.

She may not be the coolest person alive, but she sure wasn't stupid.

"They were cutting class *together*?" she asked Mr. Truman.

"That's right," he said. "I was just bringing them down to my office."

He looked so arrogant! So self-righteous.

He really was a big jerk!

She looked at Annie. "Frogs, again, I suppose?" she asked Annie.

"No, ma'am," Annie said.

"More like a snake," Abbie said, obviously thinking

87

about Truman.

"Or a dog," the senior said, obviously thinking about Scooby-Doo.

"Or an as—" I started to say, looking at our vice principal.

Before I could get the small, three-letter word out, Mrs. Caldor cut in.

"I'll handle this, thank you," she said to Truman.

"B-B-But…" he stammered. "I was going to punish them."

Punish us?

The guy was a wacko!

"I'll discipline them myself, thank you," she said to Mr. Truman.

She made her best sourpuss face. The discussion was over.

Mrs. Caldor didn't take any grief from anyone.

And *no one* questioned her.

Especially once she'd made a decision.

And she'd made a decision.

"Follow me, please," she said to all of us.

We couldn't get back into Mrs. Caldor's office from her back door. She'd obviously not brought her keys when she had rushed out.

So we had to walk around to the front of the school.

We also had to pass Mrs. Franks.

We were in single file.

Like baby ducks following their mother duck.

(Mrs. Caldor being the mother duck.)

"Hi, Annie," Mrs. Franks said when she saw Annie.

Annie waved shyly.

"Hi, Abbie," she said when she saw Abbie.

"Hey," Abbie said back.

"Andrew?" Mrs. Franks said with surprise when she saw me.

"Hi, Mrs. Franks," I said politely.

"Is everything okay at the Leeg home?" she asked Mrs. Caldor with concern.

"For now," Mrs. Caldor said with a little bit of menace in her voice.

She probably didn't want to respond until she knew the answer.

Why commit before she knew the results?

"Frogs?" Mrs. Franks asked.

"No," Mrs. Caldor said simply.

Annie, Abbie, Snoop, the senior and I piled into her office.

Then Mrs. Caldor shut the door.

"Anyone care to explain?" she asked.

She was wearing her prunella face.

We all started talking at once.

Mrs. Caldor held up her hand.

"One at a time, please," she said.

She pointed to the senior.

"You don't seem to fit in with the rest of this group," she said. "Why don't you start?"

CHAPTER 14

"Well, you see," he started off. "I took your Chia pet."

"What Chia pet?" she asked.

"The one from over there," he pointed.

She looked and nodded. "Continue."

"I'm sorry. But I've always wanted one. And you had one, and it was *dying*."

He was pleading his case well.

I say that because she didn't seem to care.

"And how are you involved in this?" she asked Snoop.

"Well, I was going to gym class and took a drink. And then I picked up the wrong backpack."

It all made sense to *us*, but I wondered how this sounded to Mrs. Caldor.

"Are you getting this?" I asked her.

She looked at me. "Not really, Mr. Leeg," she said formally. "Might you care to contribute to this befuddled story?"

I gave it a shot.

"Well, Snoop picked up the wrong backpack. Then, when he tried to return it? That guy," I pointed to the senior. "Was going berserk."

"So I didn't want to go over to him at the time,"

Snoop added.

Mrs. Caldor nodded. Her face was all squished up like a raisin. "A wise choice, I'm sure."

"Yeah, well, so then Snoop took off and I got all worried," I explained.

"You left school grounds, young man?" she asked Snoop.

Snoop paled and turned to me.

"That's not the point," I said to Mrs. Caldor.

She drew in a sharp breath. "What *is* the point?"

"Well, I guess for that part, I don't really *have* a point," I admitted.

Mrs. Caldor let her breath out slowly.

"Would someone *please* continue?" she said with little patience.

"Well, the money really freaked me out," Snoop said.

"What money?" Mrs. Caldor asked.

"The money in the Zip-Lock bag," I said.

"What Zip-Lock bag?" she asked.

"The Zip-Lock bag in the Chia pet," I explained.

"Oh yeah," Snoop added. "Sorry. But I broke your Chia pet."

Mrs. Caldor waved Snoop off. "That's all right, son."

I noticed that the senior looked heart-broken.

Snoop also noticed him. "Sorry to you, too," Snoop said to him. "I didn't mean to break it."

"He thought it was a severed head," I explained to the senior.

Mrs. Caldor gasped.

I held up my hands. "But don't worry! It wasn't. It was just the bristly, half-dead Chia pet."

Mrs. Caldor sighed loudly. "Is there a conclusion to this story?"

"Not really," I told her.

"Well, can we move on?" she asked.

"Sure," I said.

Mrs. Caldor looked from me to Abbie to Annie.

"So how are *you* involved, dear?" she asked Annie.

"Well, we were all walking home from school. And Abbie and I overheard Andrew and Snoop talking," she started to explain.

"Andrew told Snoop about how Mr. Truman burst into class," Abbie continued.

"Yeah," I added. "He was yelling at Tyrone about taking the Chia pet."

Mrs. Caldor looked at the senior. "I thought *you* took the Chia pet, Alvin."

Alvin?!

"You're name is *Alvin*?!" Snoop, Abbie and I asked the senior in unison.

"I usually go by Wolf," he said defensively.

"Isn't Alvin a chipmunk?" Snoop asked with a laugh.

The senior threw him a look.

"There's nothing wrong with the name Alvin, son," Mrs. Caldor said to Snoop. "Shall I disclose *your* real name?"

"Oh no," Snoop said. "That's okay. Alvin can be a wolf."

"So why did Mr. Truman think Tyrone took the Chia pet?" Mrs. Caldor asked me.

I shrugged. "He most likely wanted to find the missing money!"

"Yes," Mrs. Caldor said. "You mentioned money before. How much are we talking about?"

"Twenty-seven thousand dollars," Snoop, Abbie, Annie and I all said together

I thought Mrs. Caldor was going to fall out of her chair. "What?!" she said.

"Twenty-seven thousand dollars," I repeated.

"That sum will *fit* in a little knick-knack?" she cried out in disbelief.

Snoop swung his backpack around and unzipped it.

He took out the Zip-Lock baggie and handed it to Mrs. Caldor.

She stared at the small bag of money. "*This* was in the Chia pet?"

"Sho nuff," Snoop said.

She looked at Snoop.

"I don't know what to say," she said quietly.

It was a first as far as I knew.

Mrs. Caldor, in a daze.

Hm.

"I think you should call our Dad," Annie said.

"And let him investigate," Abbie added.

"We think Truman somehow stole it from the silent auction," I finished.

Mrs. Caldor looked as if we'd just hit her with a shovel.

"Mrs. Caldor?" I said quietly. "Are you okay?"

She looked at me. "Yes, this is just all so horrible."

I nodded. "Ever read the quotes of Henry David Thoreau?" I asked her.

She nodded silently. "Yes. A while ago."

"Well," I said. "*He* said, 'Rather than love, than money, than fame, give me truth.'"

Mrs. Caldor nodded. "A wise man."

"He also said 'It is never too late to give up your prejudices.'"

Mrs. Caldor looked at me and tilted her head. "How does that pertain, Andrew?"

I looked at Snoop.

So did Annie and Abbie.

"It's best if it comes from you," Abbie told Snoop.

Snoop smiled at Abbie and nodded. "The man's a bigot," he told Mrs. Caldor.

"He's a racist," I said so she'd be certain what we were talking about.

Her face turned bright red and her body started to shake. "That is intolerable!" she said loudly.

"Ask Tyrone if you don't believe me," Snoop said quickly.

"Oh," Mrs. Caldor said. "I don't doubt your word,

son."

She rose from her desk to her full height and width.

She shook with anger. "I knew of none of this!"

Then she slammed her hands down on her desk.

"He will be fired at once for his treatment of my students," she said brusquely. "And he will be investigated immediately for his thievish actions!"

And the next day? Truman was gone for good.

But not forgotten.

You'd never guess who was in charge of the fund-drive money jars.

That's right.

Truman.

And my dad also traced some stolen auction monies back to Truman.

He was skimming off the top of each donation. Then he made the big mistake of getting the large bills.

That's how my dad and his guys nailed Truman.

Everyone at school was really happy when he got fired.

They were even happier when he got caught about the money.

Tyrone especially.

And we have a few **other** series
that you might like too:

LEADER

PETE'S PLACE

THE SMITH BROTHERS

Junkyard Dan

Are you a fan?

Do you want us to put *your* comments
up on our Website?

If so, please e-mail them to:

NoxPress@gmail.com

NOX PRESS

books for that extra kick to give you more power

www.NoxPress.com